ANIMAL FRIENDS

A Collection of Poems for Children

Illustrated by

MICHAEL HAGUE

Henry Holt and Company
New York

Permission for use of the following is gratefully acknowledged:

"The Furry Ones" by Aileen Fisher from *Feathered Ones and Furry*. Copyright © 1971
by Aileen Fisher. Reprinted by permission of Marian Reiner on behalf of the Boulder
Public Library Foundation.

"Looking Around" by Aileen Fisher from *Out in the Dark and Daylight*. Copyright © 1980
by Aileen Fisher. Reprinted by permission of Marian Reiner on behalf of the Boulder
Public Library Foundation.

"My Puppy" by Aileen Fisher from *Up the Windy Hill*. Copyright © 1953, 1981 by Aileen
Fisher. Reprinted by permission of Marian Reiner on behalf of the Boulder Public
Library Foundation.

"Company" and "A Poem for You" by Adriane Frye. Copyright © 2003 by Adriane Frye.
Reprinted by permission of the author.

"The Spider's Prayer" and "The Sheep's Prayer" by Laura Godwin from *Barnyard Prayers*.
Copyright © 2000 by Laura Godwin. Reprinted by permission of the author and
Hyperion Books for Children.

"Whale Watching" and "Red Fox Afternoon" by Eileen Spinelli. Copyright © 2003 by
Eileen Spinelli. Reprinted by permission of the author.

Henry Holt and Company, LLC
Publishers since 1866
175 Fifth Avenue
New York, New York 10010
www.henryholtchildrensbooks.com

Henry Holt® is a registered trademark of Henry Holt and Company, LLC.
Compilation copyright © 2007 by Henry Holt and Company
Illustrations copyright © 2007 by Michael Hague
All rights reserved.
Distributed in Canada by H. B. Fenn and Company Ltd.

Library of Congress Cataloging-in-Publication Data
Animal friends : a collection of poems for children / [selected and illustrated] by Michael Hague.—1st ed.
p.   cm.
ISBN-13: 978-0-8050-3817-0 / ISBN-10: 0-8050-3817-5
1. Animals—Juvenile poetry. 2. Children's poetry, American. 3. Children's poetry, English. I. Hague, Michael.
PS595.A5A524 2007   811.008'036—dc22   2006018714

First Edition—2007 / Designed by Meredith Pratt
The digitally enhanced illustrations for this book were created with pencil, ink, and watercolors.
Printed in the United States of America on acid-free paper. ∞

1 2 3 4 5 6 7 8 9 10

In memory of Sue Burdick

—M. H.

CONTENTS

LOOKING AROUND   *Aileen Fisher*   7

THE SPIDER'S PRAYER   *Laura Godwin*   8

THE CATERPILLAR   *Christina Rossetti*   9

from COME HITHER, SWEET ROBIN   *Mother Goose*   10

"PEOPLE BUY A LOT OF THINGS"   *Annette Wynne*   11

from I LOVE LITTLE PUSSY   *Jane Taylor*   12

MY PUPPY   *Aileen Fisher*   15

from THE FIELDMOUSE   *Cecil Frances Alexander*   16

"HOPPING FROG"   *Christina Rossetti*   17

"WHEN THE COWS COME HOME"   *Christina Rossetti*   18

"SHOE THE HORSE"   *Mother Goose*   19

THE COW   *Robert Louis Stevenson*   20

from LOOKING-GLASS RIVER   *Robert Louis Stevenson*   22

WHALE WATCHING   *Eileen Spinelli*   23

COMPANY   *Adriane Frye*   24

RED FOX AFTERNOON   *Eileen Spinelli*   25

A POEM FOR YOU   *Adriane Frye*   26

from THE ELEPHANT   *Annette Wynne*   27

THE FURRY ONES   *Aileen Fisher*   29

THE SHEEP'S PRAYER   *Laura Godwin*   30

LOOKING AROUND

Bees
Own the clover,
Birds
Own the sky,
Rabbits,
The meadow
With low grass and high.

Frogs
Own the marshes,
Ants
Own the ground . . .
I hope they don't mind
My looking around.

—*Aileen Fisher*

THE SPIDER'S PRAYER

No rain.
Many flies.
Gentle feet
That take no notice
Of one so small.
That's all.

—*Laura Godwin*

THE CATERPILLAR

Brown and furry
Caterpillar in a hurry;
Take your walk
To the shady leaf or stalk.

May no toad spy you,
May the little birds pass by you;
Spin and die
To live again a butterfly.

—*Christina Rossetti*

COME HITHER, SWEET ROBIN

Come hither, sweet robin,
And be not afraid,
I would not hurt even a feather;
Come hither, sweet robin,
And pick up some bread
To feed you this very cold weather.

—*Mother Goose*

"PEOPLE BUY A LOT OF THINGS"

People buy a lot of things—
Carts and balls and nails and rings,
But I would buy a bird that sings.

I would buy a bird that sings and let it sing for me,
And let it sing of flying things and mating in a tree,
And then I'd open wide the cage, and set the singer free.

—*Annette Wynne*

from

I LOVE LITTLE PUSSY

I love little pussy,
Her coat is so warm,
And if I don't hurt her,
She'll do me no harm.
So I'll not pull her tail,
Or drive her away,
But pussy and I
Very gently will play.

—*Jane Taylor*

MY PUPPY

It's funny
My puppy
Knows just how I feel.

When I'm happy
He's yappy
And squirms like an eel.

When I'm grumpy
He's slumpy
And stays at my heel.

It's funny
My puppy
Knows such a great deal.

—*Aileen Fisher*

from
THE FIELDMOUSE

Where the acorn tumbles down,
Where the ash tree sheds its berry,
With your fur so soft and brown,
With your eye so round and merry,
Scarcely moving the long grass,
Fieldmouse, I can see you pass.

—Cecil Frances Alexander

"HOPPING FROG"

Hopping frog, hop here and be seen,
I'll not pelt you with stick or stone.
Your cap is laced and your coat is green;
Goodbye, we'll let each other alone.

—*Christina Rossetti*

"When the Cows Come Home"

When the cows come home the milk is coming,
Honey's made while the bees are humming;
Duck and drake on the rushy lake,
And the deer live in the breezy brake;
And timid, funny, brisk little bunny
Winks his nose and sits all sunny.

—Christina Rossetti

"SHOE THE HORSE"

Shoe the horse, and shoe the mare,
But let the little colt go bare.

—*Mother Goose*

THE COW

The friendly cow all red and white,
I love with all my heart:
She gives me cream with all her might,
To eat with apple-tart.

She wanders lowing here and there,
And yet she cannot stray,
All in the pleasant open air,
The pleasant light of day.

And blown by all the winds that pass
And wet with all the showers,
She walks among the meadow grass
And eats the meadow flowers.

—*Robert Louis Stevenson*

from
LOOKING-GLASS RIVER

Sailing blossoms, silver fishes,
Paven pools as clear as air—
How a child wishes
To live down there!

—Robert Louis Stevenson

WHALE WATCHING

The humpback whale
Bursts from the sea,
A miracle in front of me,
A rise of joy
A splash of thunder
That fills me up
With tears of wonder.

—*Eileen Spinelli*

COMPANY

Back in the woods I spot the deer.
Her ears are sharp; she knows I'm here.
Her face is shy, her legs are long.
I move too fast, and she'll be gone.

I'm shy though too, I think she knows.
That must be why she comes and goes
(and comes, and goes, and comes and goes).
That must be why—I think she knows.

—*Adriane Frye*

RED FOX AFTERNOON

Red fox, it is snowing.
Without knowing
You bless the wintry scene
Outside my door.
I watch you loping
Through my empty garden
And, watching,
Feel less lonely than before.

—*Eileen Spinelli*

A POEM FOR YOU

Bear can lumber, bear can climb.
Bear can wrestle. I can rhyme.
I'm writing you a poem, bear.
I'd step up close, but I don't dare.
Bear is furry, bear is gruff—
Pen and paper's close enough.

—Adriane Frye

from
THE ELEPHANT

The elephant is very large
And clumsy as a wooden barge,
With legs like tree-trunks, yet he's mild
And gentle as a little child.

—_Annette Wynne_

THE FURRY ONES

I like
The furry ones—
The waggy ones
The purry ones
The hoppy ones
That hurry,

The glossy ones
The saucy ones
The sleepy ones
The leapy ones
The mousy ones
That scurry,

The snuggly ones
The hug-ly ones
The never, never
Ugly ones . . .
All soft
And warm
And furry.

—*Aileen Fisher*

THE SHEEP'S PRAYER

I am just a woolly sheep.
Please help me count myself to sleep.

—*Laura Godwin*